JACK LITTLE

❖

(The No-Holds-Bard of the Hamptons)

Love-Songs
&
Graffiti

Introduced by GEORGE PLIMPTON

Illustrated by ROBERT MUNFORD

Confrontation Magazine Press
of Long Island University

Dedicated to my five children,
Lucy, David, Liza, Carl and John
with the hope that they will never
lose their sense of humor.

"Song for a Middle-Aged Man" transcribed by Ty Stroudsburg

Jack Little: Love-Songs & Graffiti
Published by *Confrontation* magazine of Long Island University

First Printing July, 1986

ISBN Number: 0-913057-08-8 (Paperback Edition)
ISBN Number: 0-913057-07-X (Limited Signed Cloth Edition)

Printed in the United States of America

Editor's Preface

This is the second volume in the occasional books series published by *Confrontation* magazine of Long Island University. This selection of light verse has received high praise by other light versifiers, among them Willard Espy, William Cole and Michael Braude. It is the first volume of poems published by the author, whose work earlier appeared in *The New York Times*, *The Reader's Digest*, *New York* magazine, and *The East Hampton Star*.

Light verse may be too general a term for the Little arsenal as he can readily switch from tongue-in-cheek to toothsome satire, from the romantic mood to a grotesque shadow-play, and from tin-pan-alley rhythms to the formal sonnet mode. With his deft balancings of light and heavy weight, he has created a new kind of poetic decorum. *Confrontation* welcomes his fresh forays into the sardonic spheres of quotidien behavior.

Martin Tucker
Editor, *Confrontation*

Introduction

Coleridge once mourned in one of his *Table Talk* essays: "I wish our clever young poets would remember my homely definitions of prose and poetry; that is, prose (equals) words in their best order . . . poetry (equals) the *best* words in the best order." What is engaging about this volume of Jack Little's is that he not only knows all about order (any man that takes on the clerihew keeps his shoes neatly lined up in his clothes closet) but that a host of his best words relate to the general area of the Hamptons . . . Temik, Claibornian dreams, the Montauk Cannonball, the Long Island Expressway, Herb McCarthy, the Barefoot Contessa, the South Fork, the potato, Sagg Pond, Guild Hall and so forth.

These words, and those that accompany them, are handled deftly, with wit and are pertinent; historians of the future who pick the South Fork for their research would do well to have a copy of *Love-Songs & Graffiti* on hand to guide them through the anthropological welter and intricacies of this place.

Moreover, as seems generic with writers of wit, Mr. Little goes after some of the inequities that annoy him, not only local but nationwide: smoking, pollution, rude drivers, fad diets. He deals with them (in controlled order, of course) with lines of savagery. Mr. Little does not pull his punches. That is appropriate enough. A minor 19th Century poet, Frederick Locker-Lampson, if you must know, produced the following lines appropriate to Little: "Some men are good for righting wrongs, — And some for writing verses". Jack Little combines both virtues in one skill — which makes him an important voice in these parts.

George Plimpton

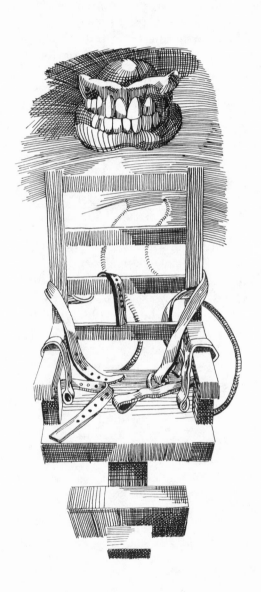

Contents

THE LUSTY LIMERICK

Limericks for Cigarette Smokers

THE WELL-MANNERED CLERIHEW

PLAYING WITH WORDS: Assorted Frivolities

DOGGERELS, CATERWAULS & BIRD SONGS

Author's Preface

The motives for writing come from many sources: the inspiration from our teachers and their teachings; our desire for preservation of experience and for our own analysis of people and events; historical reporting; translation of the human condition into the comic, poetic, dramatic and the universal; certainly the exercise of power; and, occasionally, indecent exposure.

Underlying much writing, good or bad, is the author's deep and human desire to be read and recognized during his all-too-brief existence and his hope that some of his work will survive for all time: the immortality syndrome.

I can remember archetypical conversations many years ago as an English major at Dartmouth in which I and many others would reiterate the perverse notion that it would be much more satisfactory to write one play, one poem or one novel that would go roaring down the silly ages than to make a million dollars while cruising on a private yacht with Sophia Loren mixing dry martinis in her scented stateroom — a healthy ambition in itself. Admirable as the second goal my be, it is nowhere nearly as difficult as the first, which most real writers would unflinchingly choose, though perhaps hoping to end up with both.

One of the dangerous areas of writing is attempting to be humorous, comic, or satiric without sacrificing wit. Nothing is worse than the poorly told joke, the synthetic sit-com, the heavy-handed gag or the sloppy slapstick to which deadening fallout we are constantly exposed. Real wit seems to be in short supply in our nuclear society, yet we luckily have some shining examples, both classic and modern. (Read Peter De Vries' "Consenting Adults or the Duchess Will be Furious" and find out what is meant by comic relief. It will work better than Rolaids for all symptoms of heartburn, angst and general discontent.) Read Lewis Carroll, Russell Baker, Peter De Vries, S. J. Perelman, Art Buchwald, Edward Lear, Ogden Nash, Shel Silverstein, Michael Braude. See a play by George Bernard Shaw, Neil Simon, Woody Allen. Listen to the satiric songs of Tom Lehrer and Mark Russell. Get a copy of Willard Espy's *Words at Play*. Make the acquaintance of William Cole, who wrote this immortal couplet:

"I think of my wife, and I think of Lot,
and I think of the lucky break he got."

Or see Cole Porter's *Kiss Me Kate* at least three times!

Many authentically comic authors don't depend on gag writers for their inspiration. They are the true jewelers who can take the humble stones of everyday speech and carve and polish and arrange them into brilliant new arrays. They do with words what Edward Gorey, Maurice Sendak and Charles Addams can do with a charcoal pencil — transform a grey line on a piece of white paper into an image of wit and high comedy. So, with these few perhaps self-incriminating ruminations I cautiously edge out onto the thin ice of my own humor, a frozen pond, if you will, and hazard the Mawkish Marsh, in which it is easy to get mired; the alluring Pool of Narcissus, which never freezes over; the weak, slushy areas of ice which can let one down quickly into cold water.

At least my motives are on my sleeve. I pray that a few of the odd creations in this book will strike the comic sympathies of the reader, will light small sparks of shared idiocy or love of life and language, will create small ripples of new laughter.

I am now putting on my skates . . . .

J. W. L.
Water Mill, N.Y.
June 30, 1986

Variform Verses & Versicles &
Vibrant Vignettes of
Vigorous Vintages,
Veridically
Vespine & Venturesome with
Voluptuous, Vulgar & Virile
Vocabular Vitamins.

SATIRE

The Hamptons

Rich Romans of yore would flock to Pompeii,
Politicians and pundits, the straight and the gay;
There the arriviste cream of Roman society
Would let down their hair and abandon propriety.

New Yorkers today, seeking solace and sport,
Have flooded the Hamptons, their favorite resort;
Have made it a Mecca for new millionaires
For artists and con-men and nubile *au pairs*.

All teeming with talent and money and chic,
With large cocktail parties at least twice a week,
We have playwrights and poets and publishers too,
And in August the Hamptons turn into a zoo.

Vesuvius erupted, destroying Pompeii,
The wrath of the gods, some historians say;
But the Hamptons will flourish for many a day
Until the Last Hurricane sweeps it away.

(Meanwhile, we Hamptonites love our biota
And won't think of changing it by an iota!)

A Little Steady Poisoning

The scientists have told us in no uncertain terms
That streptomycin stimulates a stronger race of germs;
And every little virus seems to grow a little wiser
When given something new to chew from Dow and Merck and Pfizer.

It seems we've been bamboozled with ecology's allure;
Our cherished race may perish if everything gets pure.
Where will all the challenge be if everything is sterile?
Let's hear it for Dow Chemical! Ignore them at your peril!

They never hurt the nematodes, the beetles seem to thrive,
Perhaps some steady poisoning will keep us all alive.
A little steady poisoning could make our genes much stronger,
A glass of Agent Orange juice might make us live much longer.

Let's drink to Union Carbide, lift a toast to old Dioxin;
Can vodka and tobacco be a timely anti-toxin?
Let's skip the boring Hamptons when we plan our next vacation,
And take a shack at Shoreham for some extra radiation.

Could New York's air pollution and the smog out in L.A.
Make city people smarter than the hicks that harvest hay?
Could acid rains improve our brains or sharpen our I.Q.s?
Perhaps carbon monoxide fumes will help our babies snooze?

Do we defeat the cockroaches, mosquitos or the rats
When we spray Raid and Warfarin and blast their habitats?
Hell no! They all get feistier (with tiny eyes a-glitter);
They come right back in healthy hordes and really seem much fitter.

So friends, let's all improve the race, as do the germs and fleas
Who seem to grow more competent when steeped in PCBs;
Let's have a tot of Temik, sprinkle Sevin in our stew,
A little steady poisoning's just the thing for me and you.

A little steady poisoning is right for you and me,
A little taste of arsenic, swordfish with mercury,
Some cute little carcinogens and yes, asbestos, too.
A little steady poisoning is just red, white and blue!

4

It's 10 p.m. Do You Know Where Your Children Are?
or Live on Channel 5

Sam is selling crack near P.S. 30,
Jennie's sniffing angel dust and glue,
Ben's ripping off some baggage at the airport
Or holding up a liquor store or two.

Hank is dealing heroin in Harlem,
Sonny's spraying paint on subway trains,
Peg is picking pockets on the buses,
Joey's snatching bags and golden chains.

Helen's busy hooking near the Waldorf,
Doing tricks with guys from out of town,
Sue's starring in a teen-age porno movie
(Wearing a transparent wedding gown).

Archie's buying gas to burn a building,
Luther's shooting up in Central Park,
Harvey's downtown beating up some faggots
Or mugging nurses walking after dark.

Phil is stealing cars for Uncle Murray,
Who turns around and sells them part by part,
Luis is being held at Riker's Island,
He stabbed his 8th grade teacher in the heart.

Frank just raped a 60-year-old lady
And killed a cop who tried to stop his car.
The judge gave him a year (he's still a minor),
To cheer him up I brought him a guitar.

Jerry's vandalizing cemeteries,
Painting swastikas on synagogues,
Bubba's burning crosses on Long Island,
Strangling cats and mutilating dogs.

So, Mr. Wise Guy, don't ask stupid questions,
I've got to meet my boyfriend in the bar.
Kids will be kids, you lousy snooping bastard,
I don't care where my goddam children are.

So, Mr. Wise Guy, no more dopey questions,
Don't give me all that foolish jive.
When I wanna know my kid's exact location
At 10, I watch them live on Channel 5!

Dedicated to John Roland

New-Trition

My grandmother told me to eat my oatmeal,
    We Scots cannot live long without it.
My uncle declared baked beans beneficial,
    In Boston there's no doubt about it.

My aunt plumped for apples, at least one a day,
    Thereby keeping the Doctor at bay.
My grandfather favored bananas and cream,
    "They're good for your tummy," he'd say.

My dad recommended a little wee nip,
    With a cold it relieves the congestion.
My mother would offer a chocolate or two
    After dinner to help my digestion.

Lovely bacon and eggs were to stoke up the fire
    So I wouldn't collapse before noon.
A well-marbled steak and devil's food cake
    Were considered both blessing and boon.

But lately I've found that these comforting foods
    Are unhealthy, old-fashioned, *outré*.
The kids say, "You're terribly out of it, Dad,
    And in danger of passing away."

What foods do they offer me morning and night
    To give gastronomical help?
Brown rice and wheat germ, rose hips and bran,
    Plus lecithin, ginseng and kelp.

They offer the pure vegetarian dinner,
    It's great when you get in the habit.
They serve raw rutabagas, raw carrots, raw beans,
    I'm beginning to hop like a rabbit.

Cholesterol's out and roughage is in,
    Beer and wine have been banned from my diet.
Coffee's forbidden, and sugar is, too,
    Here's something called "tofu," just try it!

Bottled battalions of vitamin pills
 Stand trooped in my medicine closet.
Calcium, iron and copper and zinc,
 I'm becoming a mineral deposit.

Embarked on this novel nutritional kick
 I thought all my problems would pass —
My muscles would thicken, my sex life would quicken
 And the lead disappear from my ass.

But oddly enough my life goes right on
 Without a discernible hitch,
Except now I dream Claibornian dreams!
 I'm dying to eat something rich.

In conclusion, my friends, if you suffer as I
 From family fanatics, feel free
To tell them to lump it or jump in the lake —
 Would you care to have dinner with me?

Post Haste?

They've raised the price of stamps again,
And though it's futile, I'll complain.
Will mail go faster? That's a joke
Like *post hoc, ergo propter hoc.*

For while the price of stamps grows stronger
My letters seem to take much longer.
The mail which, hare-like, used to hurtle,
Is now delivered by a turtle.

The burden of my vespine verse
Is that the U.S. Mail gets worse.
Perhaps we ought to change the vector
And send our mail by private sector?

How to Cuss Out Someone
Without Using Four-Letter Words

May you have perpetual sneezes
And chancres that fester and rot,
Ten gruesome venereal diseases,
No sex, but just teases,
Bulgarian dandruff and sniveling snot.

    May your legs be like rubber,
    Your privates decay,
    May you be epileptic, cataleptic and gray
    May your face turn to blubber,
    Your veins varicose,
    Your hair grow like cactus,
    Your colon impactus,
    And may fistulas form on the end of your nose.

May your piles multiply like the locusts,
All swarming their way up your tubes.
May you live out your life in Hohokus
With your eyes out of focus,
Drinking pig's blood and Seagrams with yellow ice cubes.

    May your bed be a'teeming
    With spiders and ants,
    May lizards and turtles crawl into your pants,
    May you scream when you're dreaming,
    With nightmares galore,
    When you murder your mother
    And bugger your brother
    And find that your wife is a two-dollar whore.

May your face resemble a gargoyle's,
May your voice be the squeal of a rat,
May your forehead be covered with boils,
May your spine grow in coils,
May a Bactrian camel defecate in your hat.

May your brain turn to jelly,
May you triple your chin,
May all your martinis be made without gin,
May gas fill your belly,
May you catch the black plague,
May you have a neurosis,
Contract psittacosis,
Insomnia, psoriasis, bilharzia, ague.

May your ulcers have tails
Made of galvanized nails,
May your off-spring be blue
and two-headed too.
May your children have troubles,
And your troubles have kids,
May your food turn to bubbles
And barbed wire and squids.

May your friends suffocate,
May your sisters abort,
May you always be late,
May your dog have a wart,
May you live in New York,
Stab your tongue with a fork,
Never quite get a cab,
Eat pizza, drink Tab,
Get mugged in the park,
Watch daytime TV,
Get raped after dark,
Get kicked in the knee.

May you slip on banana peels,
Sputum and puke
May you be the first
Under the Hydrogen NUKE!

Passing Thoughts

(I don't want to wish you any bad luck but after you cut me off on the ramp, beat me to the toll booth, passed me on the right and then gave me the finger, I couldn't help having a few uncharitable thoughts.)

May all your tires blow out simultaneously.
May your oil contain gravel and grit.
May your gas tank spring a leak when you back into a campfire.
May the wind blow your car off the George Washington Bridge.

May your brakes quit as you race up to the Grand Canyon overlook.
May 3500 Canadian geese on Ex-Lax roost overnight in your open
    convertible.
May your steering wheel come off in your hands as you zoom onto the
    Long Island Expressway.
May your glove compartment conceal several dozen starving
    tarantulas when you reach for your map.

May you sideswipe a short-tempered state trooper.
May your radio only pick up Jerry Falwell and Radio Moscow.
May your horn get stuck at your boss's wife's funeral.
May you discover, too late, a satchel of T.N.T. wired to your ignition.

May your transmission fall out as you are passing a 28-wheel trailer
    truck on a blind curve.
May the trunk of your car become the permanent home of
    10,000 killer bees.
May your headlights fail as you are going 70 mph down a steep,
    winding mountain road on a foggy night.
May a family of skunks develop a condominium in your back seat.

May you stall on a railway grade crossing with your windshield
    suddenly covered with 14 gallons of Skippy's chunky
    peanut butter just as the Montauk Cannonball comes
    SCREAMING AROUND THE BEND.

Dedicated to Johnny Carson

Hooked on Nicotine

(To be sung to the tune of "The Battle Hymn of the Republic")

Why do you keep on smoking 50 cigarettes a day?
If you keep it up like that, we'll have to call the E.P.A.
Why are you always out of breath when Johnny wants to play?
You're hooked on nicotine.

> Glory, glory emphysema,
> You'll have cancer and edema,
> You are just a foolish dreamer,
> Hello intensive care.

You're poisoning and polluting all your pulmonary sacs,
You are certainly inviting several sudden heart attacks.
Why do you keep on puffing like an engine on the tracks?
You're hooked on nicotine.

> If you want the truth, not fiction
> You have got a bad addiction.
> If you want a good prediction,
> You'll soon be off the air.

All the doctors tell you that you've got an awful hack,
The Surgeon General's warning is on every single pack,
But yet you keep on smoking even when you're in the sack,
You're hooked on nicotine.

> So, I wish you'd stop for thy sake
> And I wish you'd stop for my sake
> And I wish you'd stop for Chrissake
> If you don't stop now, beware!

Prospectus Suspectus

Of all the things in life
from which the good Lord should protect us,
high on the list, you'll agree, is the
corporate take-over or merger prospectus.

These documents often contain proposals
facetiously called "tender offers,"
which, though sounding romantic, mean,
"We want the cash in your coffers."

They also proffer the much publicized
insider leveraged buy-out,
an insidious scam which should make
any intelligent public shareholder cry out.

We may be offered subordinated debentures,
affectionately referred to as "junk,"
that could be defaulted or jettisoned
if the debt-laden ship should be sunk.

When, on TV, I see the hungry jaws
of Carl Icahn or T. Boone Pickens,
I begin to feel more and more like one of
Frank Perdue's fresh-plucked chickens.

Even though I'm now happily living
with my marvellous mistress on the Left Bank,
I think it's downright sinister that frequently
a prospectus will also stoop to such hanky-pank
as to say in an innocent, yet devious, way,
"This Page Intentionally Left Blank!"

Dedicated to Louis Rukeyser

Afraid of Freud?

(septet)
Religion is a fraud, said Freud,
This Christian nonsense I avoid
And even Jews get me annoyed.
If you crave joy quite unalloyed
Just savor being girled and boyed
And chant this mantra I've employed:
SEX IS ALL . . . THE REST IS VOID!

(clerihew)
Sigmund Freud
Was overjoyed
When patients screamed "Ouch!"
And writhed on his couch.

(narrative)
Freud would reach for a net he hid
And swoop up an ego and sometimes an id.
Then he'd relax and hum a few bars
And study the prizes he kept in small jars.

All during this time he was sending out bills
And finding new patients with baffling ills.
The money poured in, an enormous amount,
So he opened a beautiful Swiss bank account.

Then Adler told Jung and Jung told the world,
By the thousands psychiatrists' banners unfurled;
They discovered that millions of epizootics
Could be easily turned to high-profit neurotics.

They earned so much dough from their new psychic key
That they went to conventions in old Waikiki.
By perfecting this nice analytical racket
They all ended up in a higher tax bracket.

Now, in murder trials, different shrinks will maintain
A) The killer is normal. B) The killer's insane.
That's why when you go to a shrink who is clever
He'll soon have your brain more bewildered than ever.

He'll pat your patella and whisper, "Amigo,
You've got a big problem with your superego.
Have you frequently dreamed you were Oedipus Rex?
Do you have an insatiable hunger for sex?"

"Do you have penis-envy? Are you faggy or dykey?
Do you find primordial slime on your psyche?
Do you dream that you're falling? Or guilty? Or nude?
Or is your chief problem just coming unscrewed?

"Are you manic-depressive? Paranoid? Or schizo?
Take your choice and next week I'll tell you that it's so.
But if you discover another complaint,
Come back week after next and I'll tell you it ain't.

"We'll probe your subconscious and find out what's in it
(My fees are thirty-five dollars a minute).
We must dig out your deep-rooted, juvenile fears.
(A decent analysis takes several years)."

. . .

(envoi)
When you're bankrupt and feel you've been left in the lurch,
You can cheaply and quickly return to the church;
Which is why, dear beloved, you really should think:
Should you tell it to God . . . or a Freudian shrink?

SONGS OF LOVE
AND ADMIRATION

Ode to Herb McCarthy
The Squire of Bowden Square
On the Occasion of His Fiftieth Year in Business
Purveying Food and Spirits to the Elite of the Hamptons

Let's gather around and drink a toast to Herbert,
Who sells fine food from soup to roast to sherbet;
Whose Irish charm and culinary flair
Produce well-beaten paths to Bowden Square.
He knows his wines and knows his clientele,
Yet he can say (*I've heard him*) "Go to hell."
Rich or poor, Herb can't put up with phonies,
But he'll tell jokes, buy stock and play the ponies.
He's generous but he always minds the store—
I think he'd make a great ambassador!

When Herb, white waiter's coat and smile and all,
Stands at the pearly gates and gets the call,
St. Pete won't say, "I'm very pleased you came,
Just sit here at the bar and watch the game."
He'll say, "Ten thousand of your friends, old dear,
Are yelling, 'Start a new McCarthy's *here*,'
Meanwhile, please let me see your bill-of-fare—
I'll take a dry martini, oysters, roast beef, rare."
"Make mine the same," declares the Holy Ghost,
"Herb, you'll make a damn good heavenly host."

Till then . . . keep up the good work, Herb! Three cheers!
We celebrate your fifty fruitful years.

from *The Man in the White Coat* — 1986

Silly Questions

Does a baby like a tit
Does a catcher like a mitt
Does a Russian like his caviar with onions?
Does a stallion like his oats
Does a Bartlett like his quotes
Do podiatrists like athlete's foot and bunions?

Does a preacher like to pray
Does a donkey like to bray
Does an undertaker like another stiff?
Does a bee like lots of honey
Does a banker like his money
Does an Acapulco diver like a cliff?

Does a monkey like bananas
Does a smoker like Havanas
Does a mugger like a lovely golden chain?
Does a pig like eating corn
Does a cabbie like his horn
Do brain surgeons like to carve another brain?

Does a poet like a rhyme
Does a limey like a lime
Does a pitcher like to pitch a no-hit game?
Does a doggie like his bones
Does Ma Bell like telephones
Does the average moth like flirting with a flame?

Does a desert like a rain
Does a halfback like a gain
Does Billy Graham like to save a soul?
Does a cat like lapping cream
Does Alfred Hitchcok like a scream
Does Pele like to score the winning goal?

Does a fish-hawk like a fish
Does a wishbone like a wish
Does a dervish like to whirl into a dance?
Does a lioness like lions
Does a father like his scions
Does Levi Strauss like people who wear pants?

Does a Frenchman like his wine
Does Craig Claiborne like to dine
Does Johnny Carson like to entertain?
Does a vampire like his blood
Does old Noah like a flood
Does a seven-shooter like to come again?

Does a Scotsman like his scotch
Does New York like Mayor Koch
Does Hans Brinker like to glide on silver skates?
Does an Irishman like green
Do the English like their queen
Does an Arab like his camel and his dates?

When you ask, do I like you?
That's a silly question, too,
You know I like you every single way.
To conclude, do you like me?
If you like me you will see
I'd like to love you madly every day!

January Thaw

My dear, perhaps you noticed
That during my recent absence
You had a record cold spell? Zero
Degrees reached several times,
The ice boats skimming on two feet
of salt water ice. Birds frozen,
Potato fields as hard as stone.

The moment I returned, warm rain fell,
Soft south winds began to blow,
Ice melted, disappeared. Fog rose,
And the temperature hit sixty degrees.
Geese honked, happy, in the open ponds.
Trucks bogged down in the new mud.

Unseasonable, they said, not knowing
That this phenomenon,
This great thawing, has been caused
By my return to you. That my blood's heat,
My passion's warmth, my fiery expectations
of joining with your sweetness once again . . .

Have caused this spurious Spring.

To His Coy Mistress — 1986

I'm warning you!
If you don't answer my calls,
and when you do,
say you can't see me soon
because of your goddam guests from Germany;
gallery openings, garden club gatherings
and other assorted gallimaufreys;
having drinks with gallinaceous, coprophilous
pederasts whose lives consist of
decorating people to death
with lime and white chintz and wicker;
and going to fourteen fornicating fundraisers
for limousine liberals and dystopian Democrats;
and having the gall to tell me
that all this *meshuga* nonsense is IMPORTANT.
I'm warning you for the last time,
You are really screwed up, and I'll make you pay for it!

Next week I'm going to embarrass you.
I'll string a banner across Main Street
saying, "You have beautiful tits."
I will hire a plane and drag a message
along the beach from Westhampton to Montauk
reading, "I love you because you are so *zaftig*";
and then, still in the plane, I'll drop
one hundred bushels of gardenia and rose petals
all over your goddam house, and I'll
parachute packages of beluga caviar,
Scotch salmon, crisp croissants and goat cheese
from *The Barefoot Contessa* all over your goddam lawn.
What's more, I will take out full page ads
in the *N.Y. Times*, *Village Voice*, *East Hampton Star*, etc.,
saying that you are the greatest
f---- in North America . . .

Unless you call me, that is.

Song for the South Fork

April out our way is wet and windy,
and yet the shad-blow knows enough
to run out misty sprays of white
announcing Spring. The beach plum's
right behind, with showy testimonials.

It's trite to write of apple blossoms,
but I'll risk a word or two of praise
for clouds of pink and white in May,
along black branches. Nothing much sweeter
than their soft blizzard petalling the grass.

And, oh, you tempting double-bosomed lilacs,
you quintessential houris of my Spring,
nodding and preening and breathing
scented promises of Puritan nirvanas.
I bow and dig my nose in your cool fragance.

Then come meadow daisies, simple currency
of June, in drifts, in studied informality
spangling the grasses. Demure dancers
looking at the Spring in wide amaze
through symmetrical eyelashes.

Elderberry blooms on slender stems
along the woods—half in, half out—July.
Queen Anne's lace forms delicate crochets,
antimacassars for some tiny grandma's chair.
Tiger lilies stretch their tawny throats.

The orange bombs of butterfly weed
explode through August's heated meadows,
and hot, too, are the sun-gold goldenrod
standing with thick-trooped confidence,
lifting their burning plumes to scorch the air.

Then summer's end . . . September. Wild asters
waving fragile lavender goodbyes.
Pepperidge leaves, dark red
snips of shiny leather, sprinkled
on the pond in small armadas.

Now see the grand finale! Maples flaming,
brushfires of huckleberry,
sumac glowing in the Indian summer twilight,
crimson, carmine, yellow, ruby, purple,
shining in the soft October rain.

Then die we all a bit when Winter comes
withering every weed and every leaf.
And cold winds grieve around our homes,
and cold suns glint on frosted fields,
and cold moons rise from inky seas.

. . . first published in the *East Hampton Star*

A Double Sonnet
To My Son, John, Age 13
Skating in the Moonlight on Flax Pond

Like ripping silk, John tears across the ice,
His skates outlining orbits never conned.
His skates are silver shears that zig-zag slice
The black metallic fabric of the pond.
An arabesque, a leap, a hiss of power,
A whirl, a whorl, a backward hula glide,
A long, straight run. A stop—with crystal shower
That brings the sparkling show-off to my side.
My son is beautiful, my son is strong,
He imitates my cautious slip-and-slide,
His skimming and curvets make mocking song:
"Out here, old man, your son will be your guide."
The skill and exultation of this boy
Rouse envy of young muscles and young joy.

And, too, I envy him the satisfaction—
The single conquest of a single plane,
The mastery of one surface, level traction,
Without the solid geometry of pain.
He'll know, quite soon, that life has many levels
and depths and angles fearfully complex,
That men, and even women, can be devils,
And ice gets thin and people break their necks.
So, skate, John, skate! Before your brain gets sly,
Before you leave this mirror of your youth
To face the fractured prisms of humanity
Where psychedelic lights will fragment truth.
Though dubious, I wish for you smooth ice.
That you be unafraid would quite suffice!

. . . first published in the *East Hampton Star*

Poème de Terre
or Love Song to a Potato

I like them delicately boiled.
I like them French and quickly fried;
I like them baked and rissolée,
They turn me on when shepherd-pied.

I like them soufflé, au gratin,
Adore them when they're mashed and buttery.
Chowders can't begin without them,
Knishes make my heart quite fluttery.

With corned beef hash they are a must,
They yodel in a Swiss raclette;
Shoestring, scalloped or O'Brien,
My appetite is sans regret.

How lovely is a vichyssoise!
How cool, *Kartoffelen* salad!
Oh lyonnaise and dauphinoise,
You really make my stomach glad.

Solanum Tuberosum, Hail!
Despite your grotesque, warty mien,
Despite your common-garden look,
We sing to you a noble paean.

Oh face that launched a thousand chips,
To you, the fish and I do sing!
Oh flesh that lunched a thousand chefs,
You're such an unassuming thing.

I pose this question now to all,
To gourmets, pundits, Freuds and Platos—
In any civilized cuisine,
What would we do . . . without . . . potatoes?

from *The Potato Book*, William Morrow & Co., 1972
by Myrna Davis, foreword by Truman Capote

In Praise of a Shapely Lady

I can't exactly say . . . what is it
that makes your titties so exquisite?

Perhaps it's cantilevered tension
Or disbelievable suspension.

When you tittup, bouncy motions
Arouse osculatory notions.

Were I an artist, my ambition
Would be to paint your tits, like Titian.

> Were I a bird, I'd like to be
> A tit-lark in a ti-ti tree
>
> When I consider mammo-mania,
> It's plain why Oberon loved Titania.
>
> I'd climb the Grand Tetons with zest,
> My favorite port in France is Brest.
>
> Thus, when you unhook your bra,
> I can't resist an "Oooh-la-la!"

When you are near, my dear, I'm fated
To be transfixed and titillated.

I'll never see, I must admit,
A poem lovely as a tit!

Song for a Middle-Aged Man

Just like any normal man, I do everything I can
                     . . . for women!
From Florida to Maine, I'm insatiably insane
                     . . . for women!
I'm perpetually beguiled and go absolutely wild
          . . . for women, women, women, women, women!

    Oh life wouldn't be borin' next to Sophia Loren
        whose contours defy all description,
    In winter I'm warmer dreaming of Elke Sommer
        Oh doc, what a perfect prescription!
    Twould be nice if Jane Fonda would ride in my Honda
        the one where the front seat reclines,
    I'd like to count sheep close to Miss Meryl Streep
        and help her go over her lines.
    I would break every law with sweet Ali McGraw
        if she pawed me I couldn't refuse,
    I get quite unstrung when I hear Connie Chung
        deliver the NBC news!

Females make me jump with joy, cuz I'm just a growing boy
                     . . . with women!
From sea to shining sea, I enjoy propinquity
                     . . . with women!
I'm just a girlaholic who appreciates a frolic
         . . . with women, women, women, women, women!

    Oh my spirits would soar if zat Zsa Zsa Gabor
        said "Oh, yes!" and started to press me,
    I'd be at my tendrest if Ursula Andress
        undressed and said, "Baby, caress me!"
    I would lose my reserve if Catherine Deneuve
        would whisper, "Je t'aime, je t'adore,"
    I'd live in Montana if Lady Diana
        said, "Charlie's a terrible bore!"
    I would certainly fall if Lauren Bacall
        claimed that I was the man of the year,
    And in case Dolly Parton sang "When are we startin'?"
        I'd sing back, "Right away, Dolly dear!"

Song for a Middle Aged Man

John W. Little

March 1983

Just like a-ny nor-mal man___, I do ev-ery-thing I can___ for

wo-men . . . .! From___ Flo-ri-da to Maine, I'm in-

sa-tia-bly in-sane___ for wo-men . . . .! I'm per-

pe-tu-a-lly be-guiled and go ab-so-lute-ly wild___ for

wo-men, wo-men, wo-men, wo-men, wo ——— men! Oh life

would-n't be bo-rin' next to So-phi-a Lo-ren whose

con-tours de — fy all de-scrip-tion_____, In

winter I'm warm-er dream-ing of El-ke Som-mer - Oh doc, what a per-fect per-scrip-tion_____. Twould be nice if Jane Fon-da would ride in my Hon-da the one where the front seat re-clines_____. I'd like to count sheep next to Miss Mer-yl Streep and help her go o-ver her lines_____. I would break ev-ery law with sweet Al-i McGraw if she pawed me I could-n't re-fuse_____. I get quite un-strung when I hear Con-nie Chung de-

So I sing Hip Hoorah!, there's a *je ne sais quoi*

. . . about women!

As the years pass by, keep a gleam in your eye

. . . for women!

There is nothing like a dame
There is nothing quite the same
As women, women, women, women, women!

Song for a Middle-Aged Woman

Just like any normal gal, I really like to be a pal
                                   . . . with men!
I'm perpetually obsessed, and I always do my best
                                   . . . with men!
Like riding on a steed, there's something that I need
                         . . . with men, men, men, men, men!

    I'd eat garlic and scallions, to canter with stallions
        more precisely, Sylvester Stallone,
  And I'd share a hero if Robert DeNiro
        insisted that we be alone.
  I'd make love to Paul Newman, in ways superhuman
        if he'd rear back and throw me a pass,
  If I could just kitchim, I'd hitch up with Bob Mitchum
        and carefully polish his brass.
  I'd go extra innings if anchorman Jennings
        puckered up and said, "Anchors aweigh!"
  To the dogs and the kennels, I'd follow Burt Reynolds
        I'd sit up, roll over and play!

There's a feeling of the dance, starlit nights and soft romance
                                   . . . with men!
From Maine to California, I can't help from feeling hornia
                                   . . . with men!
I'm just a manaholic, who appreciates a frolic
                         with men, men, men, men, men!

  I sure wouldn't scoff, man, if cute Dustin Hoffman
        merely whispered, "Oh Baby, be mine."
  I'd call Alan Alda and sing "Falderalda,
        I want a transfusion at nine."
  I'd willingly crash with sweet Johnny Cash
        I'm sure that I'd feel right at home,
  I'd wiggle my fanny, if Marcel Mastroanni
        said, *"Carissima,* meet me in Rome."
  I might commit arson, if old Johnny Carson
        said, "I've got a great spot for you."
  And I'd act like a fool with Peter O'Toole
        his name alone gives you a clue!

So I sing Hip Hoorah! There's a *je ne sais quoi*

                                        . . . about men!
As the years pass you by, keep a gleam in your eye.

                                        . . . for men!
There is nothing like a guy
Nothing gets me quite as high

As men, men, men, men, men!

Sagaponack Sue
An Ancient Ballad of Real Estate and True Love

I'm driving out to Sue's in Sagaponack,
Lovely Sagaponack by the shore.
We will drink a quiet gin and tonic,
Or maybe two or three . . . who's keeping score?

How did I get so lucky that I'm grinning
Just like a kid with candy? Lend an ear,
I'll take you back to the beginning
And explain to you just how and why I'm here.

Sue used to be in lamps at R. H. Macy's,
But soon moved up to bras and lingerie.
She did so well with baby-dolls and panties
She summered in Sagaponack by the sea.

While renting there she purchased 30 acres
Along Sagg Pond with gorgeous water views.
I do not have to tell you — it's now priceless!
Three million bucks she'd probably refuse.

Then all the eager bachelors at Macy's
who heard about her Sagaponack score
Were after Sue like dobermans in springtime
To get a piece on Sagaponack's shore.

So Sue soon made a lovely Macy marriage
To the boy who bought the toys at Herald Square.
Too bad for her — he turned out acey-deucey.
(She soon had junior buyers in her hair.)

She shook him off just like a duck sheds water
And got her license selling real estate.
She promised she'd be a lot more careful
Selecting any new prospective mate.

She shacked up with a poet, then an artist,
Both of whom asked her for her hand,
But still Sue didn't get the message.
Guys liked her body but they *loved* her land.

The poor old poet stayed until September
When all his mother's money had run out;
The artist gave up painting in November,
Grew a beard and proved to be a lout.

So, sad old Sue put all her grief behind her
And vowed she'd never have another date.
But gentlemen kept coming to her office
Who hungered for careers in real estate.

Thus, for years and years Sue stayed celibate,
Though she was propositioned once a week
And all the urgent gentlemen who wooed her
Soon found that they were way up Heady Creek.

And that's just when I got in the picture—
I met Sue at a concert at Guild Hall,
I took her to O'Malley's for a hamburg
And didn't mention real estate at all.

It seems as though I'd pushed a magic button
When she shyly said to me, "Your place or mine?"
That night was full of moons and dunes and stardust
With my brand-new Sagaponack valentine.

Turns out that I'm a real estate attorney
Who always loved the Hamptons, don't you see.
Sue said, "You're the last step on my journey,
You're just the perfect animal for me."

So now I'm driving Sue's brand new Mercedes
And subdividing all her lovely land.
We get along like Ron and Nancy Reagan,
And life is simply fabulous and grand.

When we have kids they'll all be lawyers—
Southampton Town could always use some more.
When they graduate from Harvard Law School
They'll hang their shingles all along the shore.

• • •

So . . . I'm driving out to Sue's in Sagaponack,
Lovely Sagaponack by the shore.
We will have a quiet gin and tonic
Or maybe two or three . . . who's keeping score?

36

To Mimi Romanoff

The roar of the surf, the smell of the sea
Give us sweet feelings of tranquillity.
So when we are ready to tear out our hair,
The place to unwind is at Mimi's-sur-Mer.

Her guests are congenial and polyglot, yet
L'ambiance is *sempre gemütlich*, you bet!
So when New York City drives us to despair
We can *dolce far niente* at Mimi's-sur-Mer.

When it comes to cuisine, Mimi really inspires,
Her cooking will spark gustatorial fires.
Whenever our hunger's like that of a bear,
We'll dine like Lucullus at Mimi's-sur-Mer.

    The roar of the surf, the smell of the sea
    Give us sweet feelings of tranquillity.
    The moon on the waves, the sun on the strand,
    The long barefoot walk on the sensuous sand.

    A discourse with friends who are all polyglot,
    Skinny-dipping at midnight, *olé*, and why not?
    A sumptuous dinner of lobsters and corn
    Which can make a tired appetite quickly reborn.

When business is bleak and problems quite thistly,
We'll see Mimi Niscemi, the seeress of Sicily.
In short, to knit up the frayed sleeves of care
(to paraphrase Shakespeare), it's Mimi's-sur-Mer.

Let's give a salute to our dear Principessa,
Generous, hospitable, charming—God bless her!
Whenever our lives are dreary and bare,
We'll go roamin' off to Mimi's-sur-Mer!

Written in a Virgin Islands Guestbook

I've seen fussy chateaux on the Loire
And turreted homes on the Rhine,
I've seen castles in Spain
Where it rains on the plain,
I think that they're all very fine.

I've seen stately old homes on the Hudson
Built by Rocky and Franklin and Vin,
And English estates
With great iron gates
And a moat for the guests to fall in.

I've seen *molti palazzi* in Venice,
In Newport, a cottage or two,
I've seen large piles of brick
Raised by DuPont and Frick
Which are beautiful . . . durable, too.

But by far my favorite of favorites
(On a hill in St. Thomas, V.I.)
Is a gem and a joy
Named *Louisenhoj*,
With an outlook that dazzles the eye.

There lives our friend Carpenter Batchelder
In his tower with his orchids and such,
The kindest of hosts
With gardens and ghosts.
It's a home that I like very much.

In conclusion, I've seen many mansions
But Carpenter's castle's the best,
It's warm and has grace
A most fabulous place . . .
Regards from an old Dartmouth guest!

Montauk August Early Morning

God got out of bed on the right side this morning
and he said to Gabriel, "Bring me my heavenly glory."

"Yes, Lord," said Gabriel.

God looked at the pale, pewter-grey, watered-silk sky
in the east. He picked up his palette and brush and quickly
painted in a blush of soft magenta and muted coppery-gold.

Then God brushed the sand dunes with tawny-yellow gold dust,
stippled the beach roses shy-pink and the beach plums purple
and dusky-crimson. He touched up the whitecaps of all the
waves at sea and added foaming white petticoats to the green
waves breaking along the shore.

Then He took a handful of the very finest whitest goose down,
opened his hand and blew off long lines of soft baby clouds.

Then He took a bucket of his best Bermuda blue, threw in
some Nova Scotia high-bush blueberry-blue, some Cape Hatteras
special light jade-blue, some extra clear amethyst-blue from
the sky above the island of Mykonos as well as a bit of pure
glittery iceberg-blue from near the South Pole. He gave it
a stir and poured it out so it spread across the sky as far
as the eye could see.

Then God said, "Eureka! What a color!
Gabriel, I'm going to call it 'Montauk August Early Morning Blue.'
Don't forget how I mixed it!"

"No, Lord," answered Gabriel.

Then God breathed his gentle winds in the faces of late
sleepers and early risers, of poor and rich, of people young
and people old (the angry, the tolerant; the smug, the caring;
the oblivious, the aware; the greedy, the generous), of farmers
on their tractors in the potato fields, of fishermen putting
out to sea, of lovers entwined, of hurry-scurry humanity.
And He made the breezes spicy with the smells of salt marsh,
pine tree and bayberry.

Then God said to the sun, "Rise and shine and warm and glorify!"
And the sun obeyed.

Then God said to Gabriel, "We've done a nice job . . . I'd even
call it a work of art! Now, let's go over and hear the angels
having their morning sing."

"I'm with you, Lord," said Gabriel.

THE LUSTY LIMERICK
and Limericks for
Cigarette Smokers

The Lusty Limerick

The limerick, a peculiarly pervasive and often perverse five line rhyme (which might be called the thistle in the flower garden of poetry) had its inception in English and Irish folk and nursery rhymes in the early 1800s. It was not, however, until after Edward Lear (who was Queen Victoria's drawing teacher) published his *Book of Nonsense* that the limerick became a popular form in English-speaking countries. Lear's book was a literary milestone and soon caused limerick writing and reciting to become an English family parlor game.

Inevitably, the innocent and genteel Learical limerick lode was quickly exhausted and the English literati and university crowd began mining the more vulgar veins of sexual prowess, perversion, bodily functions, mayhem, horror and subversion. The limerick then went underground in a haze of cigar smoke and brandy fumes to emerge occasionally in surreptitiously printed collections in plain brown wrappers offered in the back rooms of bookstores or exchanged at men's clubs. Only decades later in more liberal times were the saltiest of limericks made available to the general public in English and American bookstores.

Many writers, poets, teachers, business and professional men, clergymen, U.S. presidents and British monarchs have written, swapped, collected and most certainly enjoyed the limerick. Paradoxically, salacious and uncouth limericks appeal to the most educated and sophisticated readers.

I first became hooked on this sprightly form at age 12 when my father, trying to raise my spirits while I was in bed with a fever, recited the following to me:

> I sat next to the Duchess at tea,
> It was just as I feared it would be.
> Her rumblings abdominal
> Were simply phenomenal,
> And everyone thought it was me.

Many years later, in an attempt to correct the use of "me" after "was," I composed a more grammatically acceptable version of this classic:

> I sat next to Miss Geraldine Nye,
> So embarrassed I thought I would die.
> Her ventriloqual fart
> Blew the table apart,
> And everyone thought it was I.

One of the most enduring of the limericks is:

> There was a young lady from Niger
> Who went for a ride on a tiger.
> They returned from the ride
> With the lady inside,
> And a smile on the face of the tiger.

Here is my contribution with a happier ending:

> A fluent young writer named Shepard
> Once went for a ride on a leopard.
> Though his life was in jeopardy
> Shepard's leopard-like repartee
> Made the leopard speak highly of Shepard.

. . . and another about a lady who turned the tables:

> A daring young lady from Yuma
> Disappeared on the back of a puma.
> She returned from the ride
> With a nice puma hide
> And said, "I'm not dead . . . it's a ruma."

Well-known persons who have written limericks include Rudyard Kipling, Gelett Burgess, Dante Gabriel Rossetti, Monsignor Robert Knox, Oliver Wendell Holmes, Robert Louis Stevenson, Woodrow Wilson, Morris Bishop, Carolyn Wells, Lewis Carroll, Mark Twain, and Norman Douglas. More recently, the science writer Isaac Asimov has published collections of his own limericks as has one of my all-time favorites, Edward Gorey. Like Lear, Gorey not only writes but illustrates his work.

Though I freely admit that some limericks are vulgar, even the crudest often have an appealing element of erudition. Limericks are many things: fantasies, surrealism, controlled mania, sexual acrobatics and escapades, bestiality, revolutionary statements, jolly libel and zany geography lessons. They have humor both broad and subtle; they dissect meaning and speech for shock effect and the bright-burning love of men for the wizardry of words. Limericks affirm the appreciation of alliteration, assonance, nonsense and the expression of deep desire for music in speech and laughter in Anglo-Saxon tribal rhythms.

I have written hundreds of limericks and have chosen only the following few for inclusion here. My first one is dedicated to Xaviera Hollander, author of *The Happy Hooker:*

> A talented madam named "X"
> Spread joy and made money from sex.
>   She then turned to writing
>   A trade less exciting
> But similar in many respects.*

Here are some of my others.

> Said a canny old Scot name MacLister,
> "I can't resist pleasing my sister,
>   I know it's a vice
>   But it's free and it's nice.
> She insists on incest . . . I assist her."

> Said a lusty Alaskan named Flo,
> "I love making love in the snow.
>   My husband's old engine
>   With proper attention
> Is good down to twenty below."

> In the laundry, an old opera singer
> Caught one of her tits in the wringer.
>   Her howls in high C
>   Brought back memories to me.
> In her heyday she was a humdinger.

*first published in *New York* magazine

A lady whom you'd be the first to seize
Was afflicted, alas, with the worst disease,
   It produced greenish molds
   In her wrinkles and folds
And insects in all her interstices.

There was an old fellow from Fife,
Who went to see "Jaws" with his wife.
   After the show
   He remarked, "It was so
Reminiscent of my married life."

Limericks for Cigarette Smokers

(Dedicated to the tobacco industry, their fine advertising agencies and the millions of smokaholics around the world who we hope will quit before it's too late)

There was a young man named McVay
Who smoked 62 Camels per day.
    They took out one lung
    His larynx and tongue,
Then took him entirely away.

A lady I knew from Newport
Missed the Surgeon General's report.
    Her three daily packs
    Caused acute heart attacks,
And a life that was smoky and short.

Said a heavy young smoker named Beth
Who smoked herself quickly to death,
    "My Winston tastes good
    Like a cigarette should,
Oh my God, I am quite out of breath."

Remember the Marlboro man
With his horse and his masculine tan?
    Lung cancer, edema
    And then emphysema
Made him less of a cigarette fan.

There was an old smoker named Goff
Who literally coughed his head off.
    His head rolled away
    Still puffing. I say
That Goff had some cigarette cough!

An old copywriter named Fred
Fell asleep while smoking in bed.
    As he burned to a crisp
    He cried out with a lisp,
Be Happy . . . Go Lucky . . . I'm Dead!

THE
WELL-MANNERED
CLERIHEW

The Well-Mannered Clerihew

A verse form called a clerihew is not well-known to the general public. It was invented in 1891 by a bemused English schoolboy named Edmund Clerihew Bentley. Although years later he became famous as the creator of the detective novel *Trent's Last Case*, his immortality is likely to spring from his authorship of the following four lines:

> Sir Humphry Davy
> Detested gravy.
> He lived in the odium
> Of having discovered sodium.

Bentley persisted in writing more of these gentle rhymes, and soon his friends and schoolmates, including the redoubtable G. K. Chesterton, caught the fever which spread through many of the best-known writers of the day, among them Clifton Fadiman and W. H. Auden.

So ubiquitous has this genre become that the *Oxford English Dictionary* has made Bentley's middle name, Clerihew, a general (and lowercase!) noun descriptive of the verse, surely a promulgation to make any poet proud. Here is the *OED's* summary definition: "a short comic or nonsensical verse, professedly biographical, of two couplets differing in length." The Oxford University Press, in an introduction to a Bentley collection, described clerihews more specifically and affectionately by calling them "inconsequential, usually historical, often anachronistic, always biographical . . . benignly satirical and absurdly amusing."

My own definition of a clerihew is that it is a sprightly, mildly manic, unpretentious, whimsical and biographical quatrain about the size of a black-capped chickadee. With some trepidation in speaking from such an established platform, I offer a few of my own clerihews (with a Long Island accent).

The smile of John Lindsay
Drives me to frenzy.
I lost practically all my hair
When he was Mayor.

. . .

Alexander Haig can
Eat eggs and bacon.
But his favorite meal
Is reported to be structural steel.

. . .

Ted Kennedy
Has many an amenity.
But his driving's egregious,
Particularly on bridges.

. . .

President Mitterand
Is a socialist to the bitter end.
Nonetheless, he kneels and prays
And often sings La Marsellaise.

. . .

Zsa Zsa Gabor
Has had eight husbands or more.
Which is why she is so utterly fascinating
To ladies merely sitting around waiting.

. . .

That Alistair Cooke
Has an avuncular look
Is a popular error.
On the golf course he's a holy terror.

. . .

The poetry of Robert Frost
One should read at all cost.
Even though in real life
He played God to his wife.

. . .

Admiral Hyman Rickover
Was constantly sick over
Unkind snubs
To his lovely nuclear subs.

. . .

Carl Sagan
Is not exactly a pagan.
But he claims that the Queen of Sheba
Was descended from an amoeba.

. . .

Ayatollah Khomeini
Drank one Coca Cola too many.
And while flat on his back
Was surprised by an Iraq attack.

. . .

William F. Buckley
Speaks English pluckily.
Advice to the unwary —
Bring unabridged dictionary.

. . .

Jerry Falwell
Didn't take it at all well
When he discovered his fame
Was second to that of Billy Graham.

. . .

Chairman Mao
Never kow-towed to Tao
It is said he put Buddhists
In the same category as nudists.

PLAYING
WITH WORDS:
Assorted Frivolities

A Little Espionage

Once upon a midnight crispy
When the moon's mustache was wispy,
I was drinking with my osprey
From a worn and battered frisbee,
Reading bits of Willard Espy,
Whose poems I adore.

Yes, I was reading to my osprey
(Whose nom-de-plumage is Bing Crosby),
"Osprey," I asked, "what would your guess be,
Are there grass-fed geese in Gaspé?
Does Willard Espy have great *esprit*,
Especially, *de corps*?"

Quoth the osprey (voice quite raspy)
"Rockefeller's grip is graspy,
Cleopatra's death was aspy,
There are *espaliers* in Gaspé,
Thespians daft oft in Loch Ness pee,
Espy's health! Please pour!"

Said I, "Just like the Anvil Chorus,
Espy's phonics and mnemonics
Fill us full of teasing tonics.
Compared to some, like William Shakespeare's,
Espy's verse is no great shakes, dears,
But he'll never bore us."

So, when Wede Espy goes *ad astra*,
I will pluck an aspidistra,
And when I plan his *esp*itaphing
I will write on his pilaster,
"He left us laughing."
Nil desperandum,
Nothing more.

A Travel Advisory for Foolish Birds

Any bird brain
Should abstain
From going places
Where it's plain
He's apt to suffer
Needless pain.

Even if you're
Under pressure,
Never spend the night
In Cheshire.

Do not dine
In Catalina,
You might get
A cat's subpoena.

Nor should you
Float around and gawk
While flying over
Kittyhawk.

Avoid, old chum,
The Catskill region
Lest you become
A real dead pigeon.

Barcelona's
Hostile sands
Are overrun
With Catalans.

By-pass Siam —
Those Siamese
Are crouching
In the mango trees.

If you're a sea-bird,
Never plan
To cruise upon
A catamaran.

A city all
Wise birds eschew
While near Nepal
Is Katmandu.

When you're in Rome,
St. Peter's dome
Is safer than
A catacomb.

If you're scanning
Travel tracts,
See waterfalls
Not cataracts.

When your tour guide
Mentions Manx,
Maintain your cool
And say, "No thanx."

While shopping for
A worm or frog,
Beware the shiny
Catalogue.

Russian music's
Very worryin'.
Don't relax
With Khatchaturian.

My lesson for
You birds is that
You shouldn't never
Trust a cat.

• • •

Rara avis
In vitam brevis
Cave felem
And God save us!

How to Cut Ten Minutes Off
The Time It Takes You to Do
The N.Y. Sunday Times Crossword

If you'd like to beat the crossword in a jiffy
Just memorize this doggerel, or RHYME;
Here are lots of spiffy clues
To employ or USE.
They pop up in the puzzles *all the time!*

Several ERAs or some AGEs make an EON (bet your wages!),
An odor's an AROMA, very true;
The ONAGER's an ass,
The ELAND nibbles grass,
A wildebeeste is nothing but a GNU.

An ANTE is a bet. ORE is what the miners get
Digging ADITS in an ESKER or MORAINE;
A SAMPAN is a boat,
A bit of dust, a MOTE,
A Scottish "no" is NAE, there's no gainsayin'.

You can be emphatic that oracular is VATIC,
That LAIC is a secular of sorts;
Nigerians are IBOS,
Harmless medicines, PLACEBOS,
Wrongful actions, legally, are TORTS.

Tropic plant is oft AGAVE, deserts GOBI or MOHAVE,
A RANI is a princess from Bombay;
A willow is an OSIER,
A bishop's cross a CROSIER,
A poplar is an ASPEN, in its way.

Buddhist monk is always LAMA, Chinese baby-sitter—AMAH,
A chilly northern town is doubtless NOME;
A glow is just an AURA,
A Jewish scroll, a TORAH,
Remember ERG and AMP and OHM sweet OHM.

So, when 22 across starts to throw you for a loss
And you draw a perfect blank on 40 down:
Don't start to swear, or CURSE,
Consult this RUNE, or ancient verse,
And you may win the crossword puzzle crown!

Dedicated to Eugene T. Maleska,
who has puzzled us for years.

Tongue-Twister from Aunt Felice

Dear Niece, Is Greece as nice as Nice
And are your geese still eating rice?
A piece of goose, with spice, is nice,
A slice of moose, a mousse of mice.

A peaceful lease near Nice, dear Niece,
Beats greasy rice and lice in Greece.
One can't buy geese at any price,
We cease to have polite police.

Your Auntie's knees have buckled twice,
And Uncle's cheese is hard as gneiss.
He reads *Le Monde*, grows edelweiss,
And drinks his wine on cubes of ice.

I seek surcease from skies of fleece,
From flies and fleas, the dearth of geese.
Suffice to say, dear Niece in Greece,
That life's decay is here near Nice.

You want advice, my spicy Niece,
Go find a man and treat him nice,
For ganders wander after geese.
In Nice it thunders, as in Greece.
Will wonders never cease? *Felice.*

Smatterings

I dislike the raindrop's pitter,
Tatty rats, and for that matter,
I get batty, often bitter,
Hearing feet of brats that patter.

I would rather flit than flutter,
Like to chatter more than flatter
Rather would I knit than natter,
Can't stand bits of gnats in butter.

When a putt betrays a putter,
It's far better if you mutter,
Grit or spit or even sputter
Than use gutterals from the gutter.

When your sweater's in a tatter,
Get a crafty cat, a ratter
Country cats are gritty, better;
Jet-set vets' pets apt to jitter.

When your wits are in a twitter
And you shatter every platter,
Don't forget to swat an otter
Smoking pot or kitty litter.

Write a sweaty skit on quitters,
Betters' letters, debtors' fetters
Gutsy mutts give trotters jitters,
Buy your daughter naughty setters.

When you spatter up the batter
Midst the clutter and the clatter
And your cookie cutter's glitter,
Remember — better fat than fitter.

If you stutter when she utters
Platitudes that pity potters,
Baby sitters, putty cutters,
Do not titter when she totters.

Please don't spot the family blotter,
Please don't hit her when you pat her
Don't high-hat her, try to knot her
Tit for tat. Throw roses attar!

Knock-Knock — Who's There?

Puns, some pundit once said, are the lowest form of humor. I say, with equal vigor, that "punnilingus," if I may coin a noun, may actually be the apotheosis of word play, the secret darling of the linguaphile. *Double entendre* is here to stay. Shakespeare used puns.

"Knock-Knocks," as everyone knows, are a disreputable, atrocious and flourishing genus of puns. My friend William Cole, Manhattan poet, reviewer and anthologist, is also a recognized grand punjandrum of the light verse circuit and the author of "Knock-Knocks You've Never Heard Before" and "Knock-Knocks: The Most Ever." Cole believes that the knock-knock may have originated at the famous Algonquin Roundtable, whose luminaries included Marc Connelly, Robert Benchley, Dorothy Parker and Edmund Wilson. His conclusion was reached from reading Wilson's notebooks and diary entries, *The Twenties*, in which Wilson wrote, "At one time their favorite game at the Algonquin consisted of near-punning use of words. . . . Dotty's 'Hiawatha . . . Hiawatha nice girl till I met you!' "

Cole's own favorite knock-knock (and mine) is:

>"Knock-knock."
>Who's there?
>"Amaryllis."
>Amaryllis who?
>"AMARYLLIS state agent. Wanna buy a house?"

Being something of a horticulturist, I couldn't resist coming back with a few flower pot-shots.

>"Knock-knock."
>Who's there?
>"Viburnum."
>Viburnum who?
>"You bought such nice steaks, VIBURNUM?"

"Knock-knock."
Who's there?
"Jacaranda."
Jacaranda who?
"Have you seen JACARANDA house?"

"Knock-knock."
Who's there?
"Eucalyptus."
Eucalyptus who?
"The bill for the meal is O.K. but EUCALYPTUS on the drinks."

Here are a few more atrocities from my KNOCKWURST locker.

"Knock-knock."
Who's there?
"Mazeltov."
Mazeltov who?
"I got my MAZELTOV on the Nautilus machines."

"Knock-knock."
Who's there?
"Khomeini."
Khomeini who?
"KHOMEINI fleas out of your beard today?"

"Knock-knock."
Who's there?
"Sisyphus."
Sisyphus who?
"It's Spring. When will we SISYPHUS robin?"

"Knock-knock."
Who's there?
"Dermatitis."
Dermatitis who?
"I wear Levis. DERMATITIS blue jeans."

"Knock-knock."
Who's there?
"Diefenbachia."
Diefenbachia who?
"With all the crime in New York, you never know when you have a DIEFENBACHIA."

"Knock-knock."
Who's there?
"Apocryphal."
Apocryphal who?
"APOCRYPHAL of rye."

"Knock-knock."
Who's there?
"Vertebra."
Vertebra who?
"It was so hot she didn't want to VERTEBRA."

"Knock-knock."
Who's there?
"Molasses."
Molasses who?
"MOLASSES are getting into trouble at single bars.

"Knock-knock."
Who's there?
"Herpes."
Herpes who?
"HERPES are always earlier than my peas."

"Knock-knock."
Who's there?
"Armageddon."
Armageddon who?
"ARMAGEDDON the flue, kerchoo!"

"Knock-knock."
Who's there?
"Innuendo."
Innuendo who?
"How much is the doggie INNUENDO?"

DOGGEREL, CATERWAULS & BIRD SONGS

◆

Caninedrums

(A caninedrum is a conundrum in doggerel about a dog.
The object is to read the caninedrum and then guess
what breed of dog it describes. I have not included the
answers as they are obvious.)

He's shaggy and baggy and bold
And cares not a jot for the cold.
Being quite dandy
At handing out brandy
He helps
With his yelps
In the Alps,
I am told.

      • • •

Badger hound
Sausage round
Belly rarely
Off the ground.
Name's Herman.
Talks German.

      • • •

Her nose is aquiline and thin.
At herding sheep she's jolly.
If she herded melons,
She'd be . . . melancholy?

      • • •

Quadruped maw,
Underslung jaw,
Reminds me of
My mother-in-law.
Squat and tough,
No cream puff.
If he kissed you,
What a smooch.
If he could sing
He'd be a
Whiffenpooch.

He's small and white
With hair so thick
Looks like a mop
Without a stick.

        • • •

Yips and yaps, his name is Ch'ing.
Made for laps, the worthless thing.
A bit of fluff,
A lady's muff,
A powder puff from Old Peking.

        • • •

I feel sorry for this mutt
Whose ears are clipped and tail is cut.
No wonder he's uptight and mean.
They train him to attack
And rip one up, a nasty knack.
No wonder he's not serene.
I, too, would be a grim and sober man
If I were brought up like a _____.

        • • •

There isn't a dog that is merrier
Than this tiny, silken-haired terrier.
Spry, petite, a little joy,
Twinkling feet like a wind-up toy,
Curls over her eyes, a top-knot, too,
An English pudding is the clue.

        • • •

Frisky and black but never bad,
Makes you think of half a whisky ad,
The bagpipe's skirl, Stewart plaid.
He's a terrier
But hardly a terror,
My lad.

       · • • •

This undulating lippety-lopper
Travels like a streak of copper.
You'll see him at the Irish fairs,
He often sets, but not in chairs.

. . .

This Mexican mutt
Is minuscule, but
The ladies like to kiss him.
(You could easily stir
him into your morning coffee
And never miss him).

. . .

This pug-nosed pooch with popping eyes
Is rather ugly, I surmise.
He's not at all pugnacious. Still
He'll chase a cat on Beacon Hill.

. . .

He's a showdog supreme,
A sidewalker's dream,
And his coat should really be thick.
But he's clipped so meticulously
That he comes out ridiculously —
I think it's another French trick.
With a mane on his head like a lion's,
He's apt to catch cold in his torso.
With a tuft on his tail and his ankles,
No wonder it rankles, and more so?
Tiens! C'est un chien?

A Gathering of Dogs
A Pow-Wow of Bow-Wows

. . . as guardians

a pummel of boxers
a vigil of shepherds
a pinch of dobermans
a menace of mastiffs
a snarl of attack dogs

. . . as athletes

a sprint of greyhounds
a tug of huskies

. . . as musicians

a bugle of hounds
a chorus of corgis

. . . as character actors

a primp of poodles
a goggle of pekingese
a jut of bulldogs
a majesty of great danes
a sorrow of st. bernards
a waggle of beagles
a dither of dachshunds
a droop of bassets

. . . also

a thrift of scotties
a warmth of afghans
a jet of setters
a collective of russian wolfhounds
a flicker of whippets
a dapple of dalmatians
a greeting of *ciaios*, er, chows.

Advice From My Cat

Learn to be supple,
Try to relax,
Walk as softly as melting wax.

Wash your ears
And polish your face.
Keep your claws sharpened, just in case.

Always be wakeful,
Watchful, alert,
Ready to scoot so you won't get hurt.

Act dignified,
Be patient, discreet.
When people upset you, land on your feet.

Enjoy being foolish,
Scamper and play,
Somersault, slither, slink and sashay.

Purr when you're happy,
Curl up in laps.
Make a habit of frequent naps.

Learn to be graceful,
Let yourself flow,
Walk as softly as falling snow.

The Paws That Refreshes:
A Song for Homeless Cats and Dogs

I am a little cat
Without a habitat,
Simply perishing to get to know you better.
I am cheerful (not a grouse),
I'll soon de-mouse your house,
And I'll snuggle on your oldest cashmere sweater.

> Puppies and kittens and cats and dogs
> Are tremendously loving, you see,
> So if you want a friend
> Who is faithful to the end,
> Please, please adopt me!

I am a little mutt
Without a comrade, but
If you take me in you'll find I'm rather clever.
I'll chase rabbits and I'll play,
I'll protect you every day,
And I'll be a loyal pal to you forever.

> Puppies and kittens and cats and dogs
> Are tremendously loving, you see.
> So if you want a friend
> Who is faithful to the end,
> Please, please adopt me!

I really need a family to call my very own,
I don't want to be abandoned and left alone.
So please get in your Cadillac and take a little trip—
To start us on a very warm relationship!
If you really want some tender loving company,
Come around to ARF and TAKE A LOOK AT ME!

*Dedicated to Tee Addams, Roger Caras, and my four-legged friends
at the Animal Rescue Fund of the Hamptons*

The Terrible Torrup (Snapping Turtle)

With a mouth like a trap
That is ready to snap
And a beak with a horny hook,
He's neatly concealed
'Neath a cast-iron shield
And his eyes have an evil, irascible look.

> He's the horrible, terrible,
> Simply unbearable,
> Horrible, terrible torrup;
> The voracious, predaceous,
> Distinctly rapacious,
> Horrible, terrible torrup!

He ambushes fishes
With jaws that are vicious
And gobbles up foolish frogs.
With a neck like a snake
And claws like a rake,
He cleans up the corpses of kittens and dogs.

> He's the horrible, terrible,
> Simply unbearable,
> Horrible, terrible torrup;
> The voracious, predaceous,
> Grim and ungracious,
> Horrible, terrible torrup!

He looms from the murk,
Jaws agape — with a jerk
Pulls ducklings down to their doom.
Then everything's still
As he dines on his kill
Down in the greeny-brown, submarine gloom.

> He's the horrible, terrible,
> Simply unbearable,
> Horrible, terrible torrup;
> The voracious, predaceous,
> Sly and sagacious,
> Horrible, terrible torrup!

He's ravenous, rough,
Prehistorically tough,
Baleful and menacing, dire;
And yet I am fond
Of this king of the pond;
He's a creature you have to admire.

He's the horrible, terrible,
Simply unbearable,
Horrible, terrible torrup;
Monstrous, outrageous,
Surviving the ages,
The Devil among us, the torrup!

first published in the *East Hampton Star*

Sonnet for a Crow

Oh judges all, forgive this brash debate:
I write a sonnet for the crow, a thief—
Such impudence, such gall! But here's my brief:
For crows I'll be the devil's advocate.
Sirs, I'll admit he has a Mafia style
With black silk suit of rather rascal charm.
He's sneaky, too, but with such obvious guile,
And insolent music fills his bronze alarm.
Without black crows would white doves seem as white?
Without Beelzebub, would Bibles be mere books?
Would day soon cloy without the threat of night?
Has God no eye for blackbirds, ravens, rooks?
Life's game instructs we cannot all be winners.
Sirs! Wouldn't life be dull — all saints, no sinners?

Great Grandpa Halsey's Coot Recipe

We Bonackers are still quite moot
On whether we should shoot a coot,

Or having blasted down a few,
How best to cook them—roast or stew?

Great Grandpa Halsey's recipe
Resolves this problem, as you'll see.

First, pick and clean the coots, he says,
And hang them up for several days.

And when the body leaves the neck,
It's time to cook them coots, by heck!

Next step—parboil them 14 hours
And pour the family whiskey sours.

Then lay them in a baking dish
With the head of an axe and an old dogfish.

You bake them hot all afternoon
While drinking beach plum wine, and soon

When the axe-head is fork tender
And your guests are on a bender,

Throw 'way them coots and just relax—
Serve up the dogfish on the axe!

Flaming Mamie

Flamingos, dressed in rose and pink,
Have ugly noses, don't you think?
And though bird-watchers, all a-trembling,
Come to watch flamingos dance,
I find a flamingo somehow resembling
A rather scrawny madame in a bar
(From the poorer part of France),
Gowned in a gaudy silk peignoir.

City Pigeons

City pigeons aren't adorable.
Stop to think. They're simply horrable.

They're pushy, strutty, greedy, rude
(The perfect urban attitude).

Aloft, they oft unfairly splat you
Like just another hapless statue.

Beady-eyed, this plumpish creature
Looks like Miss Gump, my eighth-grade teacher.

· · ·

The pigeon, really quite a slob,
Redeems himself if served as squab.

Say it 3 Times

Cuir pourri is French for whippoorwill,
So say it three times quickly, then be still.

Cuir pourri! cuir pourri! cuir pourri!

Now you know why to my poet's ear
It's lovely, Gallic onomatapoeia!

White Raider

When snowy owl is on the prowl,
Oh, wouldn't it be nice
To see him ghosting through the moonlight
Terrifying mice!

Goldfinch

The goldfinch doesn't fly. He swoops
And scatters gold dust as he stoops
And swings upon a thistle's head
And plucks a seed . . . his daily bread.

A Little Prayer

One hundred years from now,
Wherever we may be
(In some sweet paradise with Milton
Or some celestial harp-hung Hilton),
Good Lord, I pray, some birds allow
To keep us company.

The Sounds of Birds

I like cacaphonies of crows,
The mourning dove's seductive coo,
The cardinal's cheery whistle,
The owl's sepulchral hooting, too.

The blackbird's ringing *fleur-de-lys*,
The geese tromboning from above,
The swallow's silver gossip,
The thrush's silken song of love.

I like the laugh of lonely loons,
The Morse code of the chickadee,
The squabbling of mallards,
The whippoorwill's monotony.

Best soloist! The mocking bird
In carefree concert gets the nod.
This Pavarotti of the trees
Reveals life's inequalities
By singing every aria
With rapturous virtuoso ease
As though he were the choice of God.

Among His myriad choristers
Why did He in His wisdom vote
To put so much more music
In this small throat?

A Prayer for All of Us

May you have people to love, work to enjoy and song in your throat.

May you be blessed by rain and sun on your face, snowflakes on your eyelashes, thunder storms.

May you be a careful gardener and raise the finest fruits and vegetables and children.

May you make passionate love to a passionate lover. May you have a warm dog and a soft cat.

May you always be generous to those less fortunate, and may you have no bigotry in you.

May you read. May you hear music. May you see beauty and still understand ugliness, poverty and despair.

May you have roots in your community, staunch friends, and may you be beloved and respected in your home.

May you defend the United States of America, and may you work and pray for peace on earth.

May you praise God every day, be thankful for Nature, and ask a lot from yourself.

May you die as softly as a petal floating from an apple tree or as bravely as a spark shooting up into the darkness from a campfire.

P.S. May you realize that the best thing about life is that it is imperfect; that the best thing about humanity is that it is fallible. This leaves us all room for improvement.

The Occasional Books Series

1. *The Endless Line.* Illustrated by Alfred Van Loen
   Poetic Text by Anthony Ostroff
   Limited, signed, cloth edition $10.00
   Paper edition $6.00

2. John W. Little. *Love-Songs & Graffiti*
   Limited, signed, cloth edition $20.00
   Paper edition $7.00

3. Nancy Cardozo. *Creature to Creature*
   With illustrations by Russell Cowles
   (Expected date of publication, Spring 1987)
   Limited, signed edition $20.00
   Paper edition $7.00

Designed by Victoria Hartman
Editorial consultant: William M. Peterson
Typesetting by Packard Press, Philadelphia, Pennsylvania
Printed by Volt Information Sciences, Inc., Garden City, New York